FREAKY FABLES

FREAKY FABLES

J. B. HANDELSMAN

METHUEN

A Methuen Paperback

First published in Great Britain in 1984
by Methuen London Ltd
11 New Fetter Lane, London EC4P 4EE

This collection © 1984 J. B. Handelsman

Printed in Great Britain by
Redwood Burn Ltd, Trowbridge, Wiltshire

ISBN 0 413 55980 7

CONTENTS

These Freaky Fables originally appeared in *Punch*
and are published here by kind permission
of the editor and proprietors.

FOREWORD

In any collection of humorous work by one individual, no matter how talented, there must perforce arise differences of opinion as to the suitability and merit of the selection actually presented. This sort of crap is how forewords usually start.

Of course it doesn't really matter how they start, because nobody reads them anyway, not even the foreword writer's mother. Not even the editor, usually. Forewords are, in the purest sense of the term, completely pointless, and everybody knows it.

Which makes you a very strange person indeed to be standing there reading this. And I don't just mean deep-down peculiar, as in 'let's not join the queue right behind him'. 'Ah,' you say, 'if I am so odd, what does that make you, who actually *wrote* the bloody thing?' Simple. *I am writing this because Bud Handlesman is the best cartoonist alive.* (This is not just opinion; this is objective truth of the kind usually revealed to you only in a higher state of consciousness. And you are getting it in a foreword.)

So perhaps if you buy this book, people will think, 'Oh, he's got Bud Handelsman's new book, so he must have a good sense of humour and be OK, and not downright peculiar like they all say.' In fact, my weird friend, you had better cough up the £3.95 right now. It may be the last chance you will ever have to be accepted in normal society.

Finally, I must thank my many friends who have helped with the writing of this foreword. Without their criticism and encouragement I should many times have abandoned the whole venture. I particularly wish to acknowledge Christopher Falkus for his contribution in checking its historical accuracy, and Ann Mansbridge, who has added to her reputation as an outstanding editor by thanking me for doing it. I must also acknowledge my deep indebtedness to Daphne Day, who typed it out with willingness, despatch and no little accuracy. However, finally, of course, there is an acknowledgement to be made that is made so often by authors that it may well be in danger of being regarded as conventional. I refer, of course, to my wife. The full extent of what this foreword owes to her is immeasurable. Such merits as it may possess could hardly have found expression if she had not stopped nagging me and gone to cook supper. I am happy to be able to dedicate it to her.

John Cleese
Cap d'Antibes
Paraguay
May 1984

When You and I Were Young, Magi

ONE EVENING, THREE PRIESTS OF THE ANCIENT MEDES AND PERSIANS WERE PREPARING FOR THE WINTER SOLSTICE.

Look, boys, a star in the east!

Just in time for the holidays!

Let us follow it! Give me a minute to black up according to tradition.

The star in the east is leading us to Judaea, which is in the west.

Yuk! Yuk! Chalk up anudder miracle for ol' Zoroaster.

Oh, knock off the stereotype, Melchior.

Wise men? Sorry, King Herod already has too many of those. Any other qualifications?

Tell him we's kings.

I said knock it off.

So the King of the Jews is about to be born? What does that make **me** then, the sexton of a pickle factory?*

You are the king, of course! But he is the **KING.**

*Ancient Aramaic epigram.

Well, lots of luck! Try the nosh bar at the Bethlehem Hilton.

'Bye now.

Report back on Boxing Day at 0900 hours with exact data.

Is this the queue for the King of the Jews?

A "Behaviour", we heard, as we were abiding in the field.

A **Saviour**, dummy.

Behaviour — Saviour — as long as you're healthy.*

* Early Judaic proverb (pre-Solomon).

Manger

I'm giving nappies. What are you giving?

Just a few things we picked up at Herods.

Gold — frankincense —

— myrrh...

Wish I'd thought of that! My kids **love** myrrh.

Those stupid wise men have not come back! They were supposed to let me know which baby was the **KING.**

Why not massacre all the children in Bethlehem?

I'll have to — but it's so **messy**.

Here comes the coach. Remember, Saviours ride free.

EGYPT

Think so? Maybe they pay double.

Funny coincidence, his having the same birthday as our own Big Z.

A lot of biggies are born under Capricorn.

Somebody should have laid on a star to guide us back.

MORAL: We wish you a merry Zoroastermas, And a happy whatsit.

The Goose Girl

A FAIR PRINCESS WAS SENT TO A FAR-OFF LAND TO BE MARRIED.

I wish I could go with you, dear daughter, but this hay fever is nothing to sneeze at.

HONK

Take this soiled hanky as a magic charm.

Hurry up, we ain't got all year.

Servant girl, cut me some salami.

Here's the salami. Cut it yourself.

*In my young days, no one would have **dared** talk that way to royalty.*

Servant girl, get me some water.

Here's a cup. Get it yourself.

Where will it end? In chaos! That is my humble equine opinion.

AS THE PRINCESS BENT OVER THE STREAM, HER MOTHER'S MAGIC HANDKERCHIEF FLOATED AWAY.

My soiled charm! Help!

*Right! Now we change clothes and **I** ride the talking horse.*

I object most strenuously.

Shut up.

Don't try nothing funny, kid. I studied under Marshal Artz.

Whom?

*Hello! I had been given to understand that I was to marry a **blonde** princess.*

Oh, if I dared speak!

Yeah? Well, you been misinformed, buddy.

THE REAL PRINCESS WAS EMPLOYED AT THE CASTLE AS A GOOSE GIRL.

*There **is** something to be said for matted, filthy hair such as yours. I just can't think what it is.*

It gets like that from jogging.

HONK

Oh, don't! You remind me of my dear mother's soiled hanky.

Incidentally, would you mind bisecting my horse? He talks too m— I mean, he's like vicious.

*Oh, **no!***

My pleasure.

I am truly sorry about your head.

*Why? My head is fine — it was my **body** they cut off.*

And now fetch the prince! I am — belatedly — going to reveal all.

WHEN THE PRINCE LEARNED THE FACTS, HE HAD THE SERVANT GIRL DISEMBODIED AS WELL.

Who giveth this princess to be united in holy fetlock with this prince?

Always a bridesmaid...

I have that honour, Your Honour.

HONK

MORAL: Downward mobility is a piece of cake.

10

SHEHERAZADE

ONCE THERE WAS A SULTAN WHO MARRIED A NEW BRIDE EVERY AFTERNOON,

I do, I do—get on with it.

Imagine me—**Mrs Sultan!** It's a dream come true.

AND HAD HER EXECUTED THE FOLLOWING MORNING.

I think this is **shabby** of you.

Don't tell me how to run my business.

WHY DID HE DO THIS? FLASHBACK:

No! I'm afraid of muesli···

Eat! Or Daddy will beat you to a jelly when he comes home.

I'll let you off this time because I'm tired.

EXPLETIVE

RASPBERRY

Hit him! Hit him!

Who would be a woman? Cooking and scrubbing by day, spanking and screaming by night.

BAGHDAD GAZETTE

REVENGE

END OF FLASHBACK.

This one seems a little grotesque.

There's a shortage, I can't think why.

And will you, Sheherazade, do various things till death you do part?

I will.

I won't even wait for breakfast.

And now I'll tell you a story! Once there was a hippopotamus who was granted three wishes.

Yes, yes, go on.

Well, he ıoıoıoı and then ıuoıoıı but just at that···

···moment there came a ıuoıoı and ıuıuıoı uıııoı so anyway ıuoıoı ıuıuı good night.

NEXT MORNING

Go away! I don't know what happened to the hippopotamus.

ONE WEEK LATER

So Oedipus married his mommy and they lived together in bliss and harmony.

Goody!

Now I'll tell you one about a very naughty baboon.

IN THIS WAY SHEHERAZADE WAS ABLE TO POSTPONE HER EXECUTION FOR 1001 NIGHTS. THEN SHE CAUGHT LARYNGITIS.

Nice to be working again.

MORAL: Keep talking, and take Vitamin C.

11

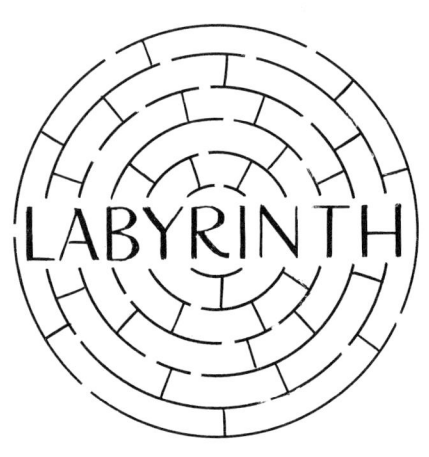

the wise pupil

IN OLDEN TIMES, WHEN INDIA'S POPULATION WAS UNDER THREE BILLION, THERE LIVED A HOLY MAN WITH HIS DEVOTED DAUGHTER.

Surely, father, you now know the sacred texts by heart.

I am not reading, Bhoona. I am only holding the book, in case anybody comes.

Is Mr Allerji at home? I desire to take holiness lessons.

He is busy pretending to read. And you are Mr—?

You may call me Vindaloo, for I am suddenly very hot.

So you wish me to be your teacher? Can you tuck your feet up like this? Without it, there can be no wisdom.

AFTER SEVERAL WEEKS

How is your spirituality coming along?

Sh! I am meditating.

Sorry.

ONE EVENING THE HOLY MAN DRANK MORE WINE THAN USUAL, AND LOST HIS TEMPER.

Fool! You don't know the Kama Sutra from the Brahmaputra!

Yes, I do—gak...

♪ I'm chantin' in the rain, ♪ just chantin' in the rain...

STILL UNDER THE INFLUENCE OF DRINK, HE CUT THE YOUTH INTO PIECES AND PUT THEM IN THE CURRY.

Not hungry?

It smells funny. The rice must have gone off. Where is What's His Name?

SUDDENLY SOBER ...

What have I done? I ate my favourite pupil! What will the gods say?

What do they usually say?

From now on this place shall be called Out of Lucknow.

Master! Let us say the prayer that brings the dead back to life! Hurry Charisma, Hurry Charisma ...

Krishna, you fool! Hurry Rama, Rama Pyjama... It is time. Daughter, cut me open.

And now I will do the same for him! Nan, chupati, puppodum, heal my master's wounded tum ...

It was very clever of you to hit on that solution when you were semi-digested.

There is not much more I can teach you, wisdomwise.

I really had to concentrate.

From now on this place shall be called Mysore.

VINDALOO AND BHOONA WERE MARRIED. BUT SHIVA, THE GOD OF DEATH, WAS ANGRY.

Damn!

MORAL: Only vegetarians should get drunk.

Tramtris the minstrel sang this story to King Arthur:

TRISTRAM and the fair iseult

KING MARK OF CORNWALL SENT HIS NEPHEW TRISTRAM TO IRELAND TO PLEAD FOR THE HAND OF PRINCESS ISEULT THE FAIR.

What a crazy name! How do you pronounce it?

Who cares? It's a political marriage.

The Irish have been troublesome lately, which is not like them at all.

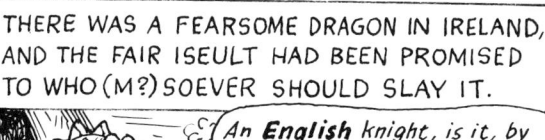

THERE WAS A FEARSOME DRAGON IN IRELAND, AND THE FAIR ISEULT HAD BEEN PROMISED TO WHO (M?) SOEVER SHOULD SLAY IT.

*An **English** knight, is it, by holy St Tyrannosaurus? Am I after eating all the Irish ones then, at all?*

He has an unfair advantage: the gift of the gab.

THE MONSTER'S FIERY BREATH MELTED TRISTRAM'S HORSE! BUT TRISTRAM LEAPED TO SAFETY AFTER FATALLY WOUNDING HIS ADVERSARY!

Ah, lads, it's a black day for poor old Buck Mulligan... Tell them — at the Green Man — that I... [Dies.]

TRISTRAM BROUGHT THE DRAGON'S TONGUE TO THE KING AND QUEEN OF IRELAND.

See, this proves I slew it.

If I didn't see it, I wouldn't believe my eyes.

Take that thing away and don't be bringing it here in the first place.

Here she is, sir: Insult the Fair.

Oh, it's not for me, it's for my Uncle Mark.

Alcohol preserve us! It's lucky for your wife you're not married.

THE QUEEN BREWED A LOVE POTION AND ENTRUSTED IT TO A FAITHFUL MAID.

This is for my daughter and King Mark, and don't be pouring it into the wrong hands.

Yes, ma'am. No, ma'am.

BUT THE MAID WAS SEASICK ON THE VOYAGE, AND TRISTRAM AND ISEULT UNSUSPECTINGLY DRANK THE POTION!

Why, this is terrible — you're beautiful!

So are you! Don't bother to answer if you can't hear me.

ALL TOO SOON, ISEULT WAS WEDDED TO KING MARK.

where is the best man?

Why? She's not marrying the best man.

Don't rub it in.

LOVE TRIUMPHED OVER HONOUR: ISEULT AND TRISTRAM OFTEN MET SECRETLY.

My darling — or should I say, my uncle's darling...

Oh, don't say a word, dearest — just let me hear you talk.

WHEN KING MARK DISCOVERED THIS, HE BANISHED TRISTRAM. THE LATTER WANDERED SADLY THROUGH THE LAND, CLOTHED IN MINSTREL'S GARB.

Don't go a-drinkin' and a-gamblin', don't go your sorrows for to drown (twang, twang): that hard-liquor place is a low-down disgrace, it's the meanest damned place in this town (twang, twang).

Tell me, Tramtris, how do you know so much about it?

Well, in point of fact I —

*Wait a minute — don't tell me — you're **him**!*

Heavens! What gave you the clue?

MORAL: It's always that last drink that does you in.

ONCE UPON A TIME, THERE LIVED **A POOR ANTIQUE DEALER** WITH HIS WIFE AND SEVEN SONS, ALL OF WHOM WERE SIX YEARS OLD EXCEPT THE WIFE.

What shall we do? Our last perfectly darling worm-eaten piece of junk has been sold.

We must cut our operating costs. We cannot afford to keep these ildren-chay.

THE SMALLEST BOY, SPENCER, WAS THOUGHT TO BE STUPID.

Why aren't you twice as big?

I don't know how.

Moron.

BUT, IN FACT, HE WAS QUITE ENTERPRISING, AND FLUENT IN PIG-LATIN.

Come along, everyone! We are going to hunt for butter churns in the forest.

I just **hate** what we're doing. It seems so **wrong**.

I just **know** I'm going to suffer the pangs of guilt for this.

Oh, do be quiet, woman.

Help! We are being deserted!

Not to worry — I knew they would do that...

... so I scattered bits of bread along the way to enable us to find our way back.

Oh, no! The birds have eaten it.

Spencer, you are a brainless imbecile!

And that's the worst kind!

Good madam, can you vouchsafe us a night's lodging?

Alas! My husband is an ogre who eats children!

But the night is freezing. Come in before you catch your death.

I smell my favourite snack — tiny tots! Where are they?

I hid them under the — I mean, what tots?

Don't lie to me, spouse, or I shall eat **you**!

AND HE DID! IT WAS **AWFUL!** THEN HE FELL INTO A DEEP SLUMBER, AND SPENCER CHOPPED HIM UP AND BORROWED HIS SEVEN-LEAGUE BOOTS, WHICH MAGICALLY FITTED HIM.

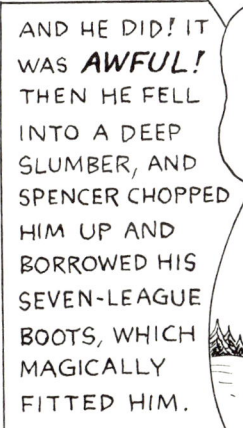

Sorry you couldn't have watched all that, but if you've seen one chopped ogre you've seen them all.

Mother! Father! We are all safe, and occupying a house filled with priceless knotty pine items, all visibly disintegrating.

Hurrah! I shall be able to afford a therapist for my guilt.

TWO YEARS LATER

What shall we do? The last adorable crumbling wreck has been sold.

You know the answer as well as I do. Get rid of the ids-kay.

MORAL: Stay with a winning formula.

15

MUTANT

SIR HUMPHREY, RETURNING FROM THE WAR—ANY WAR—WAS CAUGHT IN A VIOLENT THUNDERSTORM. WHEN HE ATTEMPTED TO FORD A RIVER, IT ROSE LIKE YEAST, AND...

...and, to make a long story short, my steed and I are going to drown. Help.

THE NEXT THING SIR HUMPHREY KNEW, HE WAS ON THE RIVER BANK, BELCHING WATER.

Egad! Marry! My call for help was purely a formality, yet it appears to have been answered.

By our lady, artificial respiration even for my mount! What manner of person is this?

I see — mute, are we? In that case I shall call you "Mutant", and, to show my gratitude, appoint you to wait upon me, hand and foot, forever.

Let us begin with foot...

THE KNIGHT AND HIS NEW SQUIRE ARRIVED AT HIS CASTLE TO BE GREETED BY TROUBLING NEWS.

Oh, sir! Your sweet wife, the lady Sadie, be deathly ill! The physicians do say as how she can be cured only with lion's milk.

INTO THE WOODS QUICKLY RAN MUTANT! WHETHER HE REALLY MILKED A LIONESS THERE, OR NOT...

...THE LIQUID WITH WHICH HE RETURNED IMMEDIATELY CURED THE LADY SADIE.

I am all better!

He be an imp of Satan! Throw him out!

WORD SPREAD THROUGHOUT THE CASTLE THAT THE SQUIRE WAS POSSESSED OF DEVILISH ARTS.

Tell us truthfully, Mutant. Are you, in fact, a son of perdition?

Zounds, you nod dumbly. Well, sorry as we are to lose your services...

...I am sure you understand that we try to run a devout — What are you doing?

MUTANT CAUGHT THE HUMPHREYS' YOUNG SON AS THE LAD FELL OUT OF A TREE.

Now I can tell all! I **was** a demon, but when I applied to be transferred they told me I could be an angel if I silently saved three humans and a horse.

This has now been accomplished, and so—

...you cannot fire me. I quit. So long.

Marry, wait a minute! What are they offering? I will double it...

MORAL: It is very hard to keep good supernatural servants.

Commerce in Canaan

The Princess Mayblossom

AT HER CHRISTENING, **The Princess Mayblossom** HAD BEEN SEMI-CURSED BY A PARTIALLY MALEVOLENT FAIRY.

When she is nineteen, she will make a really gross mistake due to inexperience.

HER PARENTS ACCORDINGLY HAD HER SHUT UP IN A TOWER WHERE SHE WAS SHIELDED NIGHT AND DAY AGAINST INEXPERIENCE.

...stepped on by a horse, rejected by leading magazines, infected with smallpox... What else is there?

Only one thing: being hit by a flying typewriter.

Happy 19th birthday!

NOW THOROUGHLY EXPERIENCED, THE PRINCESS WAS ALLOWED TO RETURN TO THE PALACE.

Mayblossom, this here gent is an ambassador from Egomania, come to request your hand for the king's son thereof.

I told him OK.

Your Highness.

*A word in your ear, Ambassador! I know nothing of your boss, but **you** are lovely beyond endurance! Shall we run away together?*

Why, Princess, I — this is most unexpected — in a word, yes.

Let us make for Puer Isle. They will never find us there.

Would you mind rowing for a bit? The diplomatic service does not develop calluses to any great extent.

THE FOLLOWING DAY:

Your Majesty, I have news of grave import.

So? Go import a grave! Business is business.

No, no...

... and they were seen making goo-goo eyes at one another, and now...

*After being horse-trampled and smallpoxed and everything, she pulls a dumb stunt like **this**?*

MEANWHILE, ON PUER ISLE:

I'm famished, woman! Why don't you fix me something to eat?

Ambassador dearest, how can you think of food? Does love not conquer all?

*It may conquer **some** things, but a growling gut ain't one of 'em.*

I picked some blueberries. We can share them.

Share them, my eye! Gulp, swallow, gulp...

All right, you, come out with your hands up!

Let me explain! I am not the ambassador but the actual prince! I came incognito to see what I was getting.

What you are getting is your head blown off.

Was he really the prince, do you think?

I hope so. Shooting ambassadors is a violation of international law.

Would you mind rowing? Kings have no muscles.

MORAL: The only thing worse than inexperience is experience.

ALI BABA,

A SELF-EMPLOYED PERSON, SAW A STRANGE SIGHT ONE DAY.

INPUT!

Thirty-seven — thirty-eight — thirty-nine —

Quite a haul today, eh, chaps?

OUTPUT!

CLANG

Why, these are Customs and Excise men!

When they have gone, I shall reclaim my overpayments.

USING THE MAGIC WORDS, ALI BABA GAINED ACCESS TO THE CAVE AND REMOVED AS MUCH LOOT AS HE COULD CARRY AWAY.

Honest fellow that I am, I took no more than was possible.

BUT ALI BABA WAS MISTAKEN! THESE WERE NO HARMLESS VATMEN, BUT DESPERADOES FROM THE INLAND REVENUE.

Someone's been in here, Chief!

Well, gentlemen, you know the next step.

Seek and destroy!

ALI BABA INNOCENTLY FLAUNTED HIS NEW WEALTH.

I don't know how I got along all these years without having my own private belly dancer.

You may start at once, Morgiana.

That's our man!

Whoopee

Ali Baba — a free-lance lint merchant! We squeezed him till he screamed! And now —

He's enjoying himself! It's sickening!

THE REVENUERS ARRIVED AT ALI BABA'S HOUSE DISGUISED AS FORTY JARS OF OIL.

Can you accommodate us?

But of course.

What luck! I'm about to take up oil painting.

MORGIANA WAS NO FOOL, HOWEVER! SHE POURED VINEGAR OVER THE VILLAINS, AND THEY PERISHED.

Presto! French dressing.

Morgiana! That's inhospitable!

I just saved your life, A.B.! That was H.M. Inspector of Taxes!

Morgiana — I am grateful beyond returns! Let me claim you as a dependant as well as a business expense.

Stop wiggling for a minute and be one of my wives.

MORAL: Don't bother with accountants. Get yourself a smart belly dancer.

CALLISTO

THE EARTH HAVING BEEN DISASTROUSLY POLLUTED, A COMMITTEE OF TWO HAS DESCENDED FROM OLYMPUS TO INVESTIGATE.

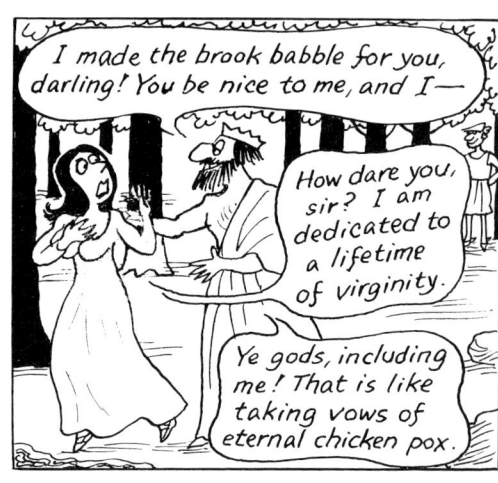

MORAL: The gods sometimes confer stardom (if that is any constellation).

The Minstrel Who Talked Too Much

(Der Geschwätzige Spielmann)

FROM THE FINALS OF THE MUSICAL TOURNAMENT AT THE THURINGIAN COURT, HERE IS MATCH POINT:

Piece of cake —

And the winner is Tannhäuser! Niece, give him the cup.

♡What ♡is ♡this ♡ ♡strange ♡feeling?♡

Von Eschenbach put up a great ballad, but he should not have sung to my forehand.

UNAWARE THAT HE HAD ALSO WON THE DEVOTION OF THE FAIR ELIZABETH, TANNHÄUSER BOOKED A WEEKEND AT THE MOUNTAIN HIDEOUT OF DAME VENUS.

I am told you sing very nicely, for a mortal.

one tries to keep in shape.

AT THE END OF A YEAR AND A DAY:

Leaving? I must be losing my touch! How can you tear yourself away?

Call it what you will— guilt — the Puritan singing ethic ...

Where have you been all this time, Tannhäuser?

All this time? Three days, at the most.

Never mind — we are having a love-song contest, the winner to get the fair Elizabeth.

♩: Love is a pure fountain ...

What do you know about it? I have rolled in the hay with Dame Venus herself.

Sacrilege!

♡Oh, ♡ ♡spare ♡ ♡him!♡

Very well — but he has to go to Rome.

Venus herself! Some people have all the luck.

TANNHÄUSER JOURNEYED TO THE HOLY CITY AND BEGGED THE POPE FOR ABSOLUTION.

After what you did? Forget it! You have as much chance of deliverance as my staff has of growing leaves.

We are pilgrims returning from Rome, lady. His Holiness forgave everybody except Tannenbaum or some such.

♡In ♡that ♡case♡ ♡I ♡will ♡now ♡ ♡die.♡ [Dies.]

Here I am, Von Eschenbach, bereaved, footsore, damned ... May as well call in on my old friend Venus.

Yoo-hoo, Tanny!

No, Tannhäuser! Love is a pure fountain, etc.

Is it? Well, I am very tired anyway. [Dies.]

MEANWHILE:

Someone bring me a new staff! This one is covered with foliage.

MORAL: People are seldom pleased to hear of other people's pleasures.

The Knight of the Bucket

THE PROUD CHEVALIER FILS D'UNE CHIENNE WAS RIDING TO SOME DEBAUCHERY OR OTHER WHEN HE REMEMBERED···

Damn! It is Good Friday! I had better confess the sins I am about to commit.

Methinks I see a holy hermit.

··· and one day last week, Holy Hermit, I broke all ten Commandments in twenty minutes. Is that a record?

You seem, my son, to lack humility.

Ridiculous! I have more humility than anybody.

As a penance, you are to crawl stark naked to St Tropez and back.

And make a bloody spectacle of myself? Why not ask me for money? I am loaded, you know.

Very well, then, fill this bucket with water and absolution is yours.

Now, **that** is what I call a terrific penance.

I have dipped and redipped this stinking bucket and every time it comes up dry and empty! I am minded to throttle that saintly man.

Enough of this foolishness! Can I give your regards to anyone in Provence?

Too late, my son, but here is a tip: Only the right sort of water will do.

FOR A YEAR THE CHEVALIER ROAMED THE EARTH SEEKING THE RIGHT SORT OF WATER, BUT ALL IN VAIN.

On to Baffin Bay.

There goes the Knight of the Bucket.

He has tried lakes, rivers, baptismal fonts, indoor plumbing, saliva···

Why, folk do say he even—

Hush! Not in front of the children.

Failure, H.H.! It is Good Friday again, and I am a lost soul. Oh, boo-hoo···

On the contrary— **success**.

See! You have shed tears of true penitence, and the bucket is filled to overflowing! You are hereby shriven.

By the way, Good Friday was in April.

They were really tears of frustration and self-pity, but any port in a storm.

MORAL: Nothing succeeds like failure.

Abe's Boys

The Singing Coachman

AFTER HIS WEDDING, POUSSIN THE COACH DRIVER IS ASKED — AS IS THE PROVINCIAL CUSTOM — TO STAY BEHIND AND SING A FEW NUMBERS.

He will be hopeless tonight — vocal cords worn out, unable to moan properly...

...qui gardait ses moutons, ron ron...

Young man, I am the Marquis de Rien, director of the Opéra. I heard you hit that high D, and you are to come to Paris at once.

But—

Sir, I appeal to you in the name of art! And also in the name of not being thrashed for disobeying a Marquis.

Fouquet, old friend, I have to go to Paris and be principal tenor. Tell Madeleine to start the connubial bliss without me.

He **what**?

Yes, Madeleine — in the name of art and of not being thrashed! But he wishes you a pleasant honeymoon and will be with you in spirit.

I thought you might at least provide my fare to Paris, Marquis.

Have you not heard of the legendary cheapness of the nobility? Drive on.

TEN YEARS LATER, MADELEINE HAS INHERITED A FORTUNE AND IS LIVING IN PARIS AS MME. SOUPÇON.

Madame, may I present our leading tenor, M. Poussin?

No one can stop you, as you are a member of the ruling class.

Are you as brainless as most tenors?

I hope so, madame. One does not like to break with tradition.

Such charm! Such wit! I shall ask her to marry me.

Fouquet, old friend, Mme. Soupçon has accepted me! But—

But you want me to pretend to be a priest so that the ceremony will lack legitimacy and you will be guilty only of adulteration and fortification rather than bigotry?

Um — yes.

The cad! He is marrying Mme. Soupçon, with whom **I** am in love! This amounts to treason!

Moreover, he already has a wife — was it not I who ruptured their relationship?

And he can't hit high D any more.

I now pronounce you this and that. You may kiss the bride.

Merci...

De rien.

No, **I** am De Rien, and this is a real priest, albeit with a false moustache! Your friend is locked in a cupboard, and the police are on their way.

You may not be a bigamist, but you **are** guilty of astigmatism.

Madeleine! How did you get here? I can explain — no, I can't...

Men! They marry you and then fall in love with the first floozie who happens to be oneself.

MORAL: Once shy, twice bitten.

The Hunter and His Wife

ONCE THERE WAS A HUNTER WHOSE WIFE WAS ALWAYS ASKING QUESTIONS.

What time is it? Have you fixed the stove? Why are you leaving? What is the capital of Baluchistan?

Nine a.m. No. Because I can't stand it. Quetta.

THE HUNTER AND HIS DOGS ROAMED ALL DAY, BUT FOUND NO GAME. FINALLY THEY CAME TO A FIRE WITH A SNAKE IN IT.

Extricate me, my good man, and you shall be well rewarded.

Grab my gun with your front paws.

Thank you! Henceforward you shall understand the language of birds & beasts.

And fish?

Not worth it. Fish make silly remarks.

But you must not tell anyone of this, or you will die!

Isn't this similar to another story?

Only superficially.

THE HUNTER CAMPED IN THE FOREST.

Think I'll trot home, Galbraith, and see how things are there.

God be with you, Friedman.

I understand every word!

LATER THAT NIGHT

Merciful heavens! What happened?

Thieves! I chased them off, but one of 'em beat me with a stick.

NEXT MORNING

May the Lord have mercy on my tiny, long-eared soul.

Damn! I can't shoot anything that prays.

Why have you returned empty-handed? How does Beethoven's 5th Symphony begin? What do you think happened last night? Who told you?

For religious reasons. Pa-pa-pa-pom. We had a burglary. I won't tell you.

Why won't you tell me?

I won't tell you why I won't tell you!

Don't you think that's outrageous? Who wrote "The Insulted and Injured"?

Yes! Dostoyevski.

UNWILLING TO SHOOT SENTIENT CREATURES, ESPECIALLY DEVOUT ONES, AND HAVING NO OTHER LIVELIHOOD, THE HUNTER FELL INTO MORBID DESPONDENCY.

I didn't reveal the secret — and yet I'm going to die! Snake!

It's not fair!

Cheer up — you're not dying of that.

What are they saying, Galbraith?

Beats me, Friedman. I don't understand people-talk.

MORAL:
Lofty principles are not rich in vitamins.

THE TWELVE TAKEOVERS OF HERCULES

A Study in Ambition

THE BUSINESS ACUMEN OF HERCULES WAS DISPLAYED AT AN EARLY AGE, WHEN HE CLEVERLY REGURGITATED HIS MILK — CREATING THE MILKY WAY FOR LATER DEVELOPMENT.

WE OFTEN READ THAT HERCULES USED A BIG CLUB. THIS IS A MISTRANSLATION. WHAT HE USED WAS A *LARGE STAFF*; WITHOUT IT, THE PAPERWORK ALONE WOULD HAVE DEFEATED HIM.

HERCULEAN TASKS, LTD.
NO JOB TOO IMPOSSIBLE

We're moving in on Nemean Lion.[1] Sound them out about a merger.

Yes, boss.

How is that? My men in the field have been **eaten**?

Hold all my calls, Miss Iphicles. I'm off to Nemea.

LATER THAT MONTH

Eeek!

A most successful amalgamation. Any problem with Hydra,[2] Iolaus?

We had a little trouble working out which head was in charge, but...

Good lad. Let me just initial the Hind[3] & Boar[4] contracts.

You want these stables deodorised in **one day**?[5]

Yes, we're having some gods round for dinner.

But a big fellow like you shouldn't be afraid of a little cow dung.

Good work, chaps, all cleansed and purified! We just diverted a couple of rivers. That comes to — deducting the value of the drowned cows...

Fraud! I'm not paying for this! You didn't even soil your fingers!

I'll see you in court.

Shoo! Shoo! Damned birds.[6]

Aren't we messing up the ecosystem, sir?

What's an echo system? This swamp will make a great shopping mall. Multi-storey car park — Sainsburyon supermarket — lots of unnecessary little tawdry shops...

At the tone, please give your name and number, preferably in Greek, and we'll get back to you. Peeeem!...

Where is your secretary — on her ouzo break? This is King Minos, in Crete. We have a fire-belching bull[7] here. It's pretty disgusting...

MORAL: Ambition's victims should be made of sterner stuff.

JOSEPH WAS SOLD TO POTIPHAR, PHARAOH'S CAPTAIN.

JOSEPH DID WELL, AND POTIPHAR WAS PLEASED WITH HIM.

AND IT CAME TO PASS THAT MRS POTIPHAR CAST HER EYES, ETC., UPON JOSEPH.

JOSEPH WAS SUCH A GREAT SUCCESS IN PRISON THAT HE WAS SUMMONED BY PHARAOH.

MORAL: Only the brave deserve the Pharaoh.

The Lute Player

THERE ONCE LIVED A KING WHO, ETC.

MORAL: Counter-tenors are irresistible.

MORAL: Thou shalt probably not commit adultery.

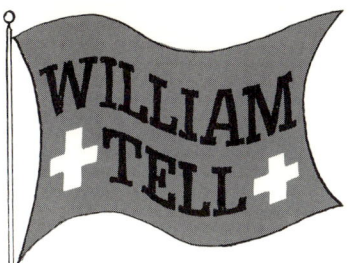

WILLIAM + TELL +

THE PEOPLE OF ALTDORF, IN THE CANTON OF URI, WERE REQUIRED TO BOW TO THE HAT OF THE AUSTRIAN TYRANT, GESSLER.

TELL WAS TO BE TAKEN TO PRISON IN GESSLER'S PRIVATE BOAT.

MORAL: When on an Alp, cover the scalp.

31

The Sigurd Saga

BRAVE KING SIGMUND'S WIFE VISITED THE BATTLEFIELD WHERE HE LAY MORTALLY WOUNDED.

Give the pieces of my broken sword to our son, that he may avenge me.

Suppose it is a daughter?

Then give them to her! I make no distinction between the sexes.

No one would expect you to, in your condition. 'Bye.

IT WAS A BOY, CALLED SIGURD. HE HAD A TUTOR NAMED REGIN.

2 + 2 = 6

Sigurd, you are no good at maths. Why do you not slay Fafnir the dragon for his hoard of gold?

See, I have repaired your father's sword. It is now the world's sharpest.

Take that, Fafnir the dragon!

Wait a mi—

BUT SIGURD LEARNED THAT REGIN (WHO, BELIEVE IT OR NOT, WAS FAFNIR THE DRAGON'S BROTHER) WAS USING HIM TO SECURE THE GOLD FOR HIMSELF.

You were planning to betray me! Is it not so?

No, I wa—

SIGURD THEN SET FORTH TO RESCUE BRYNHILD, WHO LAY IMPRISONED IN A CASTLE SURROUNDED BY FIRE.

I can ride through fire because my magic helmet makes me invisible.

Awake, Brynhild! It is I, Sigurd.

My hero!

Here, beloved, let me place this ring on your finger. I stole it from Fafnir, who stole it from his father, who stole it from a dwarf.

Oh, you darling.

It represents honour and high ideals.

SIGURD THEN RODE AWAY AND MET A LADY NAMED GUDRUN, WHOSE MOTHER WAS A WITCH.

I have given you a potion to make you forget Brynhild.

Tastes lovely! Forget whom?

Now he can marry me!

SIGURD, UNDER THE INFLUENCE OF THE POTION, RODE THROUGH THE FLAMES AGAIN.

Dearest! You have come back!

I have?

Let me replace the ring on your finger. It signifies fidelity.

It does?

SIGURD GAVE THE RING TO GUDRUN, AND MARRIED HER. AFTER THE CEREMONY, HIS MEMORY RETURNED.

Oh, no...

... and we have to write to Uncle Peter and Aunt Pam, thanking them for the carpets...

MORAL: If you find yourself in the right place, stay there.

THE SCULLERY KNIGHT

AN UNKNOWN YOUTH ARRIVED AT KING ARTHUR'S COURT WITH AN UNUSUAL REQUEST: TO BE ALLOWED TO SCRUB POTS FOR ONE YEAR.

THE KNIGHT AND THE DAMSEL WERE SUDDENLY ATTACKED BY EIGHTY-TWO ROBBERS, ALL OF WHOM WERE SOON SLAIN.

MORAL: If you can stand the heat, get into the kitchen.

THE GREAT DECEPTION

IN HIS CAPACITY AS JUDGE OF THE "MISS OLYMPUS" CONTEST, PARIS AWARDED FIRST PRIZE TO APHRODITE,

I'm told you also speak Trojan.

Hello, fans.

It's my lucky day!

What's going on? You woke me up.

WHO REWARDED HIM WITH THE GIFT OF THE WORLD'S MOST BEAUTIFUL MORTAL WOMAN: HELEN.

HELEN'S HUSBAND, THE GREEK MENELAUS, WAS DISPLEASED,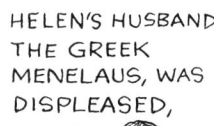

BUT THE TROJANS REFUSED TO RETURN HELEN,   AND THIS LED TO HOSTILITIES.

THE TROJAN WAR RAGED FOR MANY YEARS. IT WAS NOT A PRETTY SIGHT.

AJAX

But **I'm** a pretty sight! Right, Paris?

Yeah! Because of you, I've got to fight the whole souvlaki-eating Greek army.

You're not nice to me any more.

THE GREEKS WERE WORRIED.

We're not getting anywhere! And it's very important that we win this one.

If we lose, we'll be out of the first division.

There were hardly any spectators at the battlefield yesterday.

I have a thought! The Trojans like women, don't they?

Yes — bunch of pansies.

Well, here's my plan---

AT THE GATES OF TROY

Halt! Who are you?

A wooden horse.

A **female** wooden horse, handsome.

TOPLESS TOWERS

Well, I don't know---

Just what I've always wanted! Let it in!

WITHIN THE GATES

Yummy, gorgeous Trojan men!

Yoo hoo!

Hello, lover!

Ladies, **please**! We have a war to wage.

Not that there's any great hurry, hee-hee! That tickles.

THE TROJANS, THOROUGHLY DEMORALISED, LOST THE WAR.

He gives up.

Yeah — make love, not that other thing.

Filthy degenerate!

Nice long war, chaps. What was it about?

Can't remember.

MORAL: Beware of gifts bearing Greeks.

Guileless Fool

KING AMFORTAS, KEEPER OF THE HOLY GRAIL AND SACRED SPEAR, HAD ATTEMPTED TO USE THE LATTER AGAINST THE EVIL SORCERER KLINGSOR...

...BUT WAS DISTRACTED.

Hello, handsome! I am an arch-temptress.

Out of my way, then, and go tempt an arch.

Doesn't um want to make lovey-poo to yummy me?

SMACK!

SUDDENLY FILLED WITH LUST, AMFORTAS DROPPED THE SPEAR.

And Klingsor picked it up and stabbed him dreadfully!

Ow, ow, it hurts, it hurts...

It is said that only a guileless fool can heal the wound.

I know that!

Indeed? You're lucky I didn't **sing** it.

Hey, everybody, I shot a swan!

You what? The swans are protected here!

Oh, I do sorry.

What are you, some kind of guileless fool? ...Aha...

What is your name?

Where are you from?

Don't know.

Don't know.

It's him! They don't come any guilelesser.

THE YOUTH DONNED BLACK ARMOUR AND SET FORTH.

Yoohoo, Parsifal!

SMACK

Oh, is that my name?

I expected some lust.

Rust? But the armour is brand-new.

THE EVIL KLINGSOR THEN HURLED THE SPEAR AT PARSIFAL, WHO SEIZED IT AND MADE THE SIGN OF THE CROSS, CAUSING KLINGSOR AND HIS ENTIRE ESTABLISHMENT TO VANISH!

I like this sacred spear very much.

But I mustn't use it to poke swans. No, no, no.

MEANWHILE, AMFORTAS'S LATE FATHER HAD BEEN MAINTAINED IN A SEMI-UNDEAD STATE BY EXPOSURE TO THE GRAIL.

Uncover the grail, son. I feel myself growing deader.

I can't, dad. My old injury is acting up.

THIS REFUSAL CAUSED THE DECEASED KING TO EXPIRE.

Here I am! Allow me to touch your wound with this saintly weapon.

Be careful, you guileless fool!

Holy mackerel, I'm healed ...Unveil the cup!

Too late.

I was in thrall for my sins to the wicked sorcerer, but now, thanks to you, I can die.

My pleasure, ma'am.

Bury her with me! I may be dead, but I ain't too old.

MORAL: Ye shall become as little children, or worse.

The Private Patient

THE SYRIANS HAD DESCENDED IN THEIR MIGHT UPON THE ISRAELITES AND SUCCEEDED IN CAPTURING A LITTLE GIRL…

… WHO SERVED THE WIFE OF NAAMAN, CAPTAIN OF THE SYRIAN HOST.

Why so sad, Mrs?

Alas! My husband is a leper! He dareth not go out in the rain, lest it dissolve the glue that secureth his nose.

In my country we have a prophet who cureth anything, even death.

Thou dostn't say!

IN DUE COURSE, THE KING OF ISRAEL RECEIVED A LETTER FROM THE KING OF SYRIA.

He asketh **me** to cure this man's leprosy? I, who cannot even get rid of my own cold?

Clearly, he cocketh another snook against Israel.

Read this provocation, Elisha. Should I take the Golan Heights? Behold, I rent my clothes.

From whom?

Never mind, leave it unto me.

NAAMAN WAS SENT TO THE HOUSE OF ELISHA THE PROPHET.

My master prescribeth seven baths in the river Jordan.

Baths? The quack! Why doth he not come out and lay his hands upon me?

What, and catch it himself?

Baths in Jordan, eh? This is war! We will wipe the floor with these people, maybe even capture another little girl.

Begging pardon, sir, but why not do it? Washing is not hard.

No? Hast thou ever tried it?

Bath number seven … It worketh! Behold, I am as clean as a whistle!

Elisha, my nose runneth over! How much?

No charge, my dear fellow, thou wert treated on the Theological Health.

Hmm.

THE SERVANT OF ELISHA WAS GREEDY.

Oh, Naaman! My master forgot — the surgery is normally closed to the public on Thursdays.

So how much doth he want?

Oh, let me see… Make it a lot.

Whence comest thou?

Nowhence.

Which way to the river Jordan?

Never try to fool a doctor, thou dummy! We also **give** diseases.

MORAL

36

FOR REASONS OF STATE,

FRANCESCA DA RIMINI

IS ENGAGED TO BE MARRIED TO GIOVANNI MALATESTA, NICKNAMED "THE DISGUSTING".

SHORTLY THEREAFTER, A FIERCE BATTLE RAGES BETWEEN THE GUELPHS AND THE GHIBELLINES.

IN NEED OF SOLACE, FRANCESCA READS ALOUD FROM HER FAVOURITE ROMANCE, "TOM SWIFT AND HIS WATER-POWERED WASTEBASKET", AS PAOLO THE GORGEOUS ENTERS UNNOTICED.

MORAL: Ugly does as ugly is.

THE DWARF'S BLESSING

Once upon a time, a widow had a beautiful, nasty daughter and a plain, charming stepdaughter.

THE WOMAN HATED HER STEPDAUGHTER FOR BEING SO GOOD AND KIND.

You! Go out in the snow, wearing nothing but paper underwear, and pick strawberries.

Yes, stepmother.

Heh heh! She'll freeze.

Surely my stepmother knows there are no strawberries — and I am very cold in my paper lingerie — hello?

Give me half of your lunch.

Take it all, if you like cat food.

Good girl! See, your basket is full of strawberries! And from now on, whenever you open your mouth, a gold coin shall fall out.

Oh, thank you, sir!

Here are the strawberries.

But you were supposed to freeze to death!

What went wrong?

Are you really spitting gold? I think I'm losing my mind.

WHEN THE STEPMOTHER UNDERSTOOD WHAT HAD OCCURRED, SHE SENT HER OWN DAUGHTER OUT, HOPING FOR THE SAME GOOD FORTUNE.

Ah, here comes the little twerp.

Give me half of your lunch.

Share my scampi meunière with you? You've got to be kidding, runt.

Bad girl! No strawberries! And whenever you speak, a toad shall jump out of your mouth.

Oh, yeah? Says who?

You and your bright ideas!

What is the world coming to? Is there no injustice?

WHEN SUMMER CAME, THE STEPDAUGHTER WAS SENT OUT TO CHOP WOOD.

And see that you cut off at least three fingers, or it will go hard with you.

Yes, stepmother dear.

Stop the coach! That young woman has just expectorated a sovereign.

I am the King, my dear. Will you be my Queen? I shall not conceal from you that the enormous benefit to the royal treasury is part of my motivation.

I accept.

*Wait a minute! What about **this** girl? Isn't she lovely?*

Be seductive, stupid.

Hello there, Your Majesty.

Fine! I'll take that one as well! Have you got one who spits books? I love to read.

Shall I bring my axe?

Jane Austen would not have permitted such a dénouement.

Why don't I mind my own business?

MORAL: Don't play dwarf.

Sir Pelleas,

HAVING OUTJOUSTED ALL OTHERS AT THE CAERLEON FINALS, WAS AWARDED THE COVETED CIRCLET (RATHER LIKE A SMALL CROWN OR LARGE NAPKIN RING).

I now place this gadget upon the matchless head of the most beauteous Lady Catarrh.

Bumpkin!

Lady, why do you treat me thus? I love you.

If you do not stop following me, I shall call the police.

But I defeated the police in the tournament.

EVERY DAY, SIR PELLEAS MAINTAINED HIS VIGIL OUTSIDE THE CASTLE OF THE WOMAN WHO DESPISED HIM.

Moan! Moan! She refuses to love me! Moan!

Jenkins, throw another load of garbage on yon knight.

Sir Pelleas, is it not? Sir Gawain here. I have heard of your plight and I sympathise no end.

I have a plan. Wait behind yon tree.

SIR GAWAIN'S PLAN WAS TO REPORT TO THE LADY CATARRH THAT HE HAD SLAIN SIR PELLEAS, IN ORDER THAT HER HEART MIGHT BE SOFTENED.

You slew him? Marvellous! Did he bleed a lot, I hope? Stay for dinner.

What a divinely callous person.

NOW IT WAS SIR GAWAIN'S TURN TO FALL IN LOVE.

Alas, I have waited three weeks behind this tree, and I begin to fear for the life of my loyal friend.

STEALTHILY, SIR PELLEAS CREPT TOWARDS THE CASTLE.

But soft — I hear voices.

How brave you are! Let me feel your biceps.

Let me feel yours.

Hee-hee! Those aren't biceps, silly.

Deceived! Betrayed! Should I kill them both?

No — that would be unknightly.

So what?

I think I am going to be sick.

DETERMINED TO TAKE TO HIS BED AND NEVER RISE AGAIN, SIR PELLEAS CHANCED TO MEET THE LADY NIMUE (SHE WHO HAD LEARNED OCCULT ARTS FROM MERLIN HIMSELF) AND RECOUNTED HIS STORY.

Is that all? Leave it to Nimue! Wait behind yon tree.

Please — not yon tree.

NIMUE'S SPELLS PRODUCED RADICAL CHANGES IN ALL CONCERNED PARTIES.

You could easily curdle cream! Do you charge by the quart?

I feel nothing but disdain for you and your stupid biceps! It is Pelleas I love!

Now I hate Lady Catarrh, and I love *you*! Why could all this not have been arranged sooner?

You are a bigger person for having suffered, dear heart.

Am I? Hot dog.

MORAL: Things are never so bad that they cannot be helped by a little magic.

39

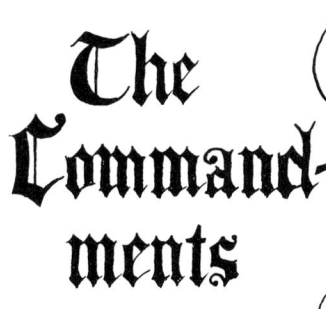

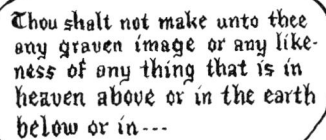

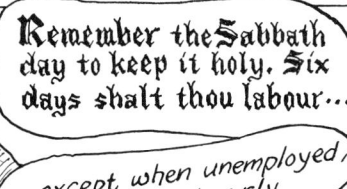

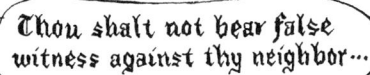

MORAL: Keep the commandments, perhaps in a locked box with other important documents.

The Youth Who Was Unacquainted with Fear

THERE ONCE LIVED A COUPLE WHOSE SON WAS SO STUPID THAT NOTHING FRIGHTENED HIM.

Hello, mummy.

Boo!

Grrr...

Is that you, dad?

It's hopeless.

He doesn't get it from me! My family were Quakers.

Nor from me! I remember my father — there was nothing that man wasn't afraid of.

THE DISAPPOINTED PARENTS EXPELLED THEIR SON.

And don't come back until you've been scared out of your wits like all decent folks!

What wits?

Maybe I should apprentice myself to a master trembler.

THE YOUTH HAD MANY ADVENTURES, WHICH HE FACED WITH HIS USUAL MINDLESS COURAGE.

ROARGLP.

Could I be missing an enzyme? Then again, what is an enzyme?

Sir, can you direct me to the Royal College of Fear?

Boo! They won't admit you. You either got it or you don't got it. However...

THE KINDLY STRANGER SENT THE YOUTH TO SEE THE KING.

So you have never mastered the art of flinching? Boo! No, I see you haven't.

I have a job for someone in your underprivileged condition.

THE YOUTH WAS ASSIGNED TO GUARD A HAUNTED CASTLE.

Boo!

Boo!

Boo!

(Yawn)

We'd better try something stronger than "boo", chaps.

Now you shall die!

Oh, I don't think so.

You tripped me! That isn't fair.

I'm sorry. Are you hurt?

Not really. Just embarrassed.

We know when we're licked! Tell the King the curse is lifted.

The cellar is full of money. Help yourself.

If you see Sir Keith, tell him we said hello.

Good work, lad! Here is my daughter, whom you will now have to marry.

Hi.

I have a funny feeling, which I suspect may be fear.

MORAL: We have nothing to fear but fearlessness.

41

THE ENCHANTED PIG

ONCE UPON A TIME, A FAIR PRINCESS WAS TOLD HER FORTUNE.

Are you sure?

Alas, yes! The tarot cards, the tea leaves, the baconlike stripes intersecting your district line, all tell the same story: You will marry a pig.

IN DUE COURSE, A VISITOR ARRIVED AT THE ROYAL PALACE.

Hail, O King! May your life be prosperous and filled with garbage.

Would you believe, without my glasses I thought for a moment you were a— my God, you **are**.

But look here, I can't let my daughter marry you! It's, well, how shall I put it, not kosher.

Take care! I am not alone! Do you not hear all that oinking in the courtyard?

I'm afraid you have no choice! However, his grammar is excellent, for a pig, and he may well be enchanted.

Enchanté, my dear.

See?

AND SO THEY WERE MARRIED.

Now, bridegroom, take the ring from the Best Pig and jam it on your bride's left trotter.

JUST LINKED

Look at all that mud! Stop the coach! I really **must** have a wallow.

Ah, that was lovely... Give us a kiss.

Like total degradation.

THE NEXT MORNING

Welcome to brecky, husband! I must say, you didn't behave at all piggishly last night. In the dark, I almost thought—

Well, we can't always be at the top of our form. Ah! Scrambled swill.

LATER THAT DAY

Hello! I believe you have an enchanted husband. I can fix that, but it will cost you.

Name your price!

THAT NIGHT

Why do you want me to take these pills?

To release you from your curse, silly! Did you think I didn't know?

It worked! I used to turn into a man at night, but **that** won't happen any more, praise Hog! Give us a big slobber.

Why couldn't I have let disgusting enough alone?

MORAL: Let sleeping pigs lie.

Caesar and Cleopatra and Antony and Cleopatra

merlin in love

THE LADY OF THE LAKE CAME ONE YULETIDE TO THE COURT OF KING ARTHUR ACCOMPANIED BY HER TWELVE SISTERS.

How nice to see all of you! Until today I have beheld only your right arm sticking out of the lake.

I know! Thank heaven for holidays, is what I say.

THE YOUNGEST OF THESE WAS THE LADY NIMUE, BY WHOM THE WISE MERLIN WAS MUCH AFFECTED.

Her hair is like a corrugated tin roof—her eyes are the colour of wild strawberries...

Moon... moon...

Pull yourself together, man! You are much too venerable for this sort of thing.

You forget that I am living backwards.

Only this morning two of my teeth fell **in**.

Yes, back to the lake, unfortunately! Just as I was beginning to dry off... But I am concerned for Nimue.

Many thanks, dear lady, and be assured in turn of **my** concern for nim **you**.

MERLIN, MEANWHILE, WITH NIMUE'S HELP, WAS MAKING A PERFECT ASS OF HIMSELF.

You little fool, do you not know what is in my heart?

Valves, right? We had that in biology.

What I really want to learn is black arts and things.

Presto! The dog is now a cat! A mouse! A fish! An onion! A dog again! Am I doing it right?

This is the most confusing day of my life.

Such an apt pupil! How I adore you.

WHEN AT LAST SHE LEFT THE COURT, MERLIN WENT WITH HER. ONE DAY THEY CAME TO A HUGE ROCK.

Inside the rock, dearest, is an auto-harp. It plays itself, thus making it unnecessary to hire musicians.

Darling—your lips are like hips...

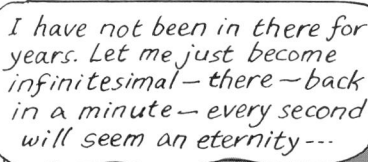

I have not been in there for years. Let me just become infinitesimal—there—back in a minute—every second will seem an eternity---

Presto! The opening is sealed! Did I do it right?

Hey!

Just in time, too. Things were getting rather nauseous.

YEARS LATER

Funny about Merlin, Guinevere, the way he just left and never came back.

He was always a bit unstable.

By now, of course, he would be too young to be of much use.

MORAL: Try not to make yourself too small.

THE TWO COATS

CAUGHT IN A FEARFUL STORM AT SEA, THE QUEEN OF HUTSYPLUTS AND THE SHIP'S CAPTAIN PLACED THEIR RESPECTIVE INFANT SONS IN A CHEST WHICH THEY THREW OVERBOARD.

Sorry, the chest holds only two.

THE SHIP THEN SANK THOROUGHLY.

SEVENTEEN YEARS LATER

Tell us the facts of life, mum and dad! Where do babies come from?

Well, Otto and Grotto, some folks say they emanate from the tummy...

...but in our experience they seem to come from the chest.

A SAILOR WHO HAD SURVIVED THE SHIPWRECK, ONLY TO FALL VICTIM TO AMNESIA, RECOVERED HIS WITS AT ABOUT THIS TIME AND RELATED WHAT HAD OCCURRED.

Hence I, the king, am going from house to house seeking two lads who were formerly in a box.

But they are ours! We found them on our own beach.

THE FOSTER-PARENTS WERE REWARDED BY BEING ALLOWED TO CONTINUE RECEIVING FAMILY ALLOWANCES, AND THE BOYS WERE BROUGHT TO THE PALACE.

But which is my son, wise old councillor? Both have my soulful eyes and my late wife's adorable conk.

Leave it to wise old me.

Your Highness and the other kid, you are to wear these gold-embroidered velvet poofy coats for six months and **never take them off.**

Their condition will then tell me which of you is the prince.

OTTO AND GROTTO WERE VERY CAREFUL NOT TO SOIL THEIR PRETTY COATS, AS EACH HOPED TO BE JUDGED THE PRINCE.

Here comes an unruly horse, Grotto!

Help! My lovely coat will be trampled!

Oh, thank you, sir! That was truly heroic.

But it hasn't done me any good, coatwise.

THREE MONTHS LATER OTTO INTERVENED TO PREVENT TWO IRATE LADIES FROM BEATING A GENTLEMAN TO DEATH.

Grab the swine by the coat while I slug him, Millicent.

Please, madam! Not by the coat!

Ah, sir, you have earned my dying gratitude.

SHORTLY BEFORE THE FATEFUL DAY, OTTO SAVED A CHICKEN FROM DROWNING.

And now the damned coat will shrink.

To say nothing of the chicken droppings.

Grotto, your coat is as splendid as ever! Otto, yours looks as if it had been spread across a puddle for three overweight ladies in spiked boots.

Four, actually.

Hail to the rightful prince, who cares only for appearance! Obviously you were born to govern...

My son.

...whereas your foster-brother is fit only to be a sea captain or a social worker.

Not that...

MORAL: Altruism is the natural enemy of elegance.

ENGLAND WAS IN TERRIBLE SHAPE WHEN GOOD KING

Richard the Lion-Hearted

ASCENDED THE THRONE.

INTRODUCTIONS IN THE HOLY LAND

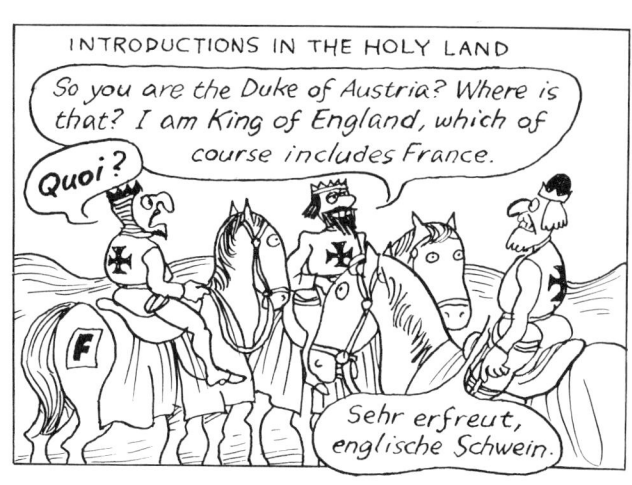

RETURNING HOME OVERLAND, RICHARD WAS ARRESTED FOR TRESPASSING.

BLONDEL THE MINSTREL ROAMED EUROPE, SEEKING HIS MASTER.

HIS RANSOM PAID, RICHARD RETURNED TO ENGLAND WHERE, IN MONK'S GARB, HE WENT TO INVESTIGATE THE NOTTINGHAM-SHIRE CRIME WAVE.

RICHARD WAS SLAIN WHILE FIGHTING AGAINST HIS FORMER ALLY, THE KING OF FRANCE.

MORAL: Some prefer artichoke hearts.

ANTI-SLEEPING BEAUTY

ONCE UPON A TIME THERE LIVED A LOVELY PRINCESS NAMED AURORA.

SHE HAD BEEN BLESSED WITH BEAUTY, WEALTH, AND FREEDOM FROM TOOTH DECAY.

What else can we give her?

What about intelligence?

No, no! She may have to rule the country some day.

BUT SHE HAD ALSO BEEN CURSED.

By the time this kid hits 16, she goes to **sleep**.

And I don't just mean R.E.M. —I mean the real **deep stuff**.

TO AVERT THE CURSE, AURORA WAS SENT TO LIVE IN THE WOODS, AND FORCED TO STAY AWAKE UNDER AN ASSUMED NAME.

ONE DAY...

What are you called, my dear?

Cosima Elfenbein, but I'm not allowed to lie down or talk to strangers.

I wish I could spirit you away, Cosima, but I am a handsome prince and my father is taking me into the business and you know how it is.

Moreover, I can never remember the erogenous zones.

Farewell, dear one.

ON HER SIXTEENTH BIRTHDAY, AURORA WAS RETURNED TO HER PARENTS.

Happy birthday to you, hap—

Arnold, look! She's gone to sleep!

Z

It's the **curse**!

Everybody to bed! I'll call Rent-a-Prince.

If they're closed, try Wake-the-Dead Road Repairs, Ltd.

Faster!

I don't know why I'm doing this! I am in love with Cosima Elfenbein.

Give her a big wet kiss —quick!

It's **her**! Stand back, everybody!

Z

No, no, on the mouth—that's it.

SMACK

Curses! He found it.

Some people have no consideration! I've been up for sixteen years, and the minute I— oh, it's you.

THEY WERE MARRIED AND LIVED HAPPILY EVER AFTER.

What do you think, Cosima? Britain may soon have a general election.

Z

MORAL: Insomnia—now, **that's** a curse.

47

The Wooing of GUINEVERE

GOOD KING UTHER PENDRAGON, KNOWING HIMSELF TO BE AFFLICTED WITH TERMINAL DYSLEXIA, BEQUEATHED A CIRCULAR ITEM TO HIS FRIEND, KING LOUDGROAN.

Bit large, isn't it?

Certainly! It has to be, to feed 250 chaps.

WHEN LOUDGROAN WENT TO WAR, HIS BEAUTIFUL DAUGHTER OFTEN SERVED AS HIS PAGE.

Do me up in the back, Guinevere. I can never reach the final button.

There! You look very chic, daddy. Your foes will be terribly impressed.

ONE DAY, WHEN THE TIDE OF BATTLE WAS RUNNING AGAINST GOOD KING LOUDGROAN...

Get the fop!

Help!

The louts! Sartorial elegance is wasted on them.

...OF A SUDDEN THERE APPEARED IN THE FRAY AN UNKNOWN KNIGHT, SO SMARTLY ATTIRED THAT GUINEVERE FELL INSTANTLY IN LOVE WITH HIM.

High fashion and St George!

Take that! And that! And this!

He is winning for us! But who is he?

And where does he buy his lovely designer armour?

Sir, you have earned a place at the Dart B— I mean the Round Table! Daughter, sizzle up an extra burger 'n' bun for the stranger.

Such hair! Like finely spun 100% cotton.

But before eating, you must take the vow! Repeat after me: "I solemnly promise to hit ladies very seldom..."

AFTER THE GINGER NUTS

Ah, what an Epicurean repast! Care for another milk shake? Ask and it shall be given. Incidentally, who are you?

*I am hight Arthur, King of Britain (outranking **you**, by the way)— and even more than a milk shake I desire your fair daughter.*

Plus the table, which was my old man's.

By all means, take the lot! Anything else? How are you fixed for clean underwear?

SOME YEARS AFTER GUINEVERE HAD BECOME ARTHUR'S QUEEN, A RESPLENDENTLY CLAD NEWCOMER RODE INTO CAMELOT.

Who may you be, dapper sir?

Launcelot of the Lake, London and Paris. May I serve you?

Cheeky! You may, indeed.

MORAL: **Chiv'-al-ry,** *n.* The state or condition of being a clothes horse.

The Purple Cat

ONCE UPON A TIME, A QUEEN WHO OWNED A WHITE CAT DREAMED OF A PURPLE CAT.

We must have that purple cat! The man who finds it shall be our bride — we mean... Pardon us, we are still half asleep.

SUITORS TRAVELLED EVERYWHERE IN SEARCH OF THE PURPLE CAT (FOR THE QUEEN WAS GREATLY DESIRED BOTH FOR HER WEALTH AND HER PERFECT TEETH).

Worth a cool zillion, I'd say.

And those incisors! You couldn't get a piece of dental floss between 'em.

Here, kitty! Never mind — not purple enough.

A year has sped, Prime Minister, and we are still purple catless.

I advocate harsh measures, ma'am.

We agree! Announce the decapitation of all citizens in alphabetical order.

Excellent idea! My name is Zygote, and I am very old anyway.

AN OBSCURE YOUNG DENTIST NAMED ACKROYD WAS ALARMED.

All the Aarons and Abiyoyos are gone! There is not a moment to lose.

Bad News HOPELESS QUEST PURPLE CAT RESULTS IN STEW

Luckily, I am an experienced catnapper.

THE FOLLOWING MORNING

Here is the purple feline of which Your Majesty dreamt.

Our hero!

We know very little about dentistry, our dear. We have never had a cavity in our life.

Never mind, darling. I shall give you one on each birthday.

AFTER THE WEDDING, THE CAT (BEING INTOXICATED) LOST HER FOOTING ON THE ROOF AND FELL INTO THE MOAT.

Your purple cat, ma'am.

That is our **white** cat! We see it all now!

Summon the Prince Con-Man at once.

You didn't say it had to be **permanently** purple — and I am too young to die.

But not to **dye**, scoundrel! You are now the Court Painter, than which nothing is lower.

Last night we dreamt of a chartreuse cat. Get busy.

MORAL: Water colour is a treacherous medium.

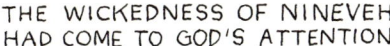
THE WICKEDNESS OF NINEVEH HAD COME TO GOD'S ATTENTION.

JONAH TRIED TO FLEE FROM THE PRESENCE OF THE LORD.

THE LORD SENT A GREAT WIND, AND THE SEA WAS TEMPESTUOUS, AND THE MARINERS WERE AFRAID.

THE MEN FINALLY BECAME CONVINCED THAT JONAH WAS RESPONSIBLE FOR THE ROTTEN WEATHER.

JONAH SPENT THREE DAYS IN A FISH.

SEEING THAT JONAH WAS PROPERLY CONTRITE, THE LORD SPAKE UNTO THE FISH.

AND JONAH'S MISSION WAS A GREAT SUCCESS;

AND THE PEOPLE OF NINEVEH REPENTED, AND THE LORD SPARED THEM.

MORAL: Few of us are improved by having been sea-food.

Waking Beauty

AS EVERYONE KNOWS, THE PRINCESS AURORA WAS AWAKENED BY A KISS FROM PRINCE CHARMING, AND THEY WERE MARRIED. NOW READ ON *(IF YOU LIKE)*.

THE PRINCE WAS NOT ASHAMED OF HIS BRIDE; ON THE CONTRARY, HE WAS ASHAMED OF HIS MOTHER, WHO WAS AN INCURABLE OGRESS.

AS KING, CHARMING COULD NO LONGER MAINTAIN HIS FAMILY IN SECRECY.

ONE DAY, KING CHARMING WAS INVITED TO WAR BY A NEIGHBOURING MONARCH.

THE COOK SUBSTITUTED TOAD MEUNIÈRE AND VERMIN PROVENÇALE, SO CLEVERLY DISGUISED THAT THEY TASTED LIKE HUMAN MEAT. BY THE THIRD DAY, THE QUEEN MOTHER BELIEVED SHE HAD EATEN HER SON'S ENTIRE FAMILY.

MORAL: It is almost impossible to poison some people.

The Sultan Shish-al-Kebab

WAS IN THE HABIT OF WALKING ABOUT AT NIGHT, DISGUISED AS A MARKET RESEARCHER. HE WAS THUS ENABLED TO PEER AT THE POPULACE WITHOUT AROUSING HOSTILITY.

Sisters, let us fantasise! I wish I worked at the royal palace.

So do I.

Work? *I* wish I were the Sultan's **wife**! I would — Who is that at the window?

Nobody — only the market research man.

THE FOLLOWING DAY, THE SISTERS WERE SUMMONED TO THE THRONE ROOM.

Being omniscient, I am fully aware of your foolish fancies of last night.

Forgive us, O All-Wise One!

Do not attack us with tongue depressors!

I would not **dream** of torturing such lovely creatures during the holy month of Ramadan! Some other time, perhaps! Instead, I shall grant your wishes.

You and your "Let us fantasise"!

You and your "So do I"!

Meanwhile, our sister Amphora, that lucky slut, shares the All-Wise One's bed.

LATER THAT YEAR

Over-eating, are we, Amphora dear?

Only pickles! The Court physician is almost certain that I am with tot.

How nice! You must let us grab it as it emerges.

WHEN THE BABY WAS BORN, THE JEALOUS SISTERS PLACED IT IN A BASKET AND SET IT ADRIFT IN THE CANAL, WHERE IT WAS FOUND BY AN ITINERANT MANAGEMENT CONSULTANT.

By Allah, an authentic baby! The wife will be terribly pleased.

She gave birth to a **puppy**? How is that possible?

Alas, noble sir, it is caused by a recessive gene! We have several uncles who bark.

And a cousin who rotates three times before going to bed.

THE SAME THING OCCURRED WHEN THE SECOND CHILD ARRIVED.

A **cat**?

Our aunt licks herself all over.

AND THE THIRD.

A **sheep**?

Our grandfather was extremely woolly.

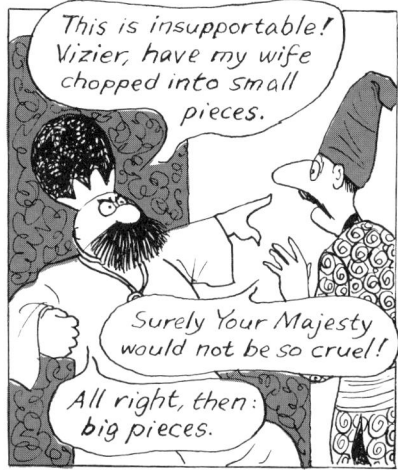

This is insupportable! Vizier, have my wife chopped into small pieces.

Surely Your Majesty would not be so cruel!

All right, then: big pieces.

AS IT WAS AGAIN RAMADAN, AMPHORA WAS NOT MINCED, BUT INSTALLED IN THE MOSQUE TO BE SPAT ON DAILY BY THE FAITHFUL.

And the children grew up to be management consultants. Night-night.

But, Sheherazade — did the king never find out? Were the evil sisters not punished? Was the queen not exonerated?

Alas, my husband, no, no, and no! This is a **true** story.

MORAL: Never reveal your inmost thoughts in the presence of market research.

Kidnapped!

THE KING AND QUEEN OF CODSWALLOPIA WERE SKILLED IN ALL THE ARTS.

ONE DAY, WHEN THE KING WAS BUSY IN THE PRINTMAKING WORKSHOP, THE QUEEN WAS ACCOSTED IN THE FOREST BY A STRANGE KNIGHT.

THE FOLLOWING MIDDAY, THE KING ACCOMPANIED HIS WIFE TO THE SPOT WHERE SHE HAD MET THE KNIGHT.

* The queen thought of these words several centuries before Keats.

FOR MONTHS THE KING DWELT IN THE FOREST, EATING BERRIES AND TWIGS AND CHARMING THE WOODLAND CREATURES WITH HIS MUSIC AND GRAPHICS.

A BIRD ARRIVED ONE DAY WITH USEFUL INFORMATION.

THE KING PENETRATED THE FAERIE FASTNESS, AND PERFORMED FOR THE COURT.

MORAL: "We only part to meet again."
— John Gay.

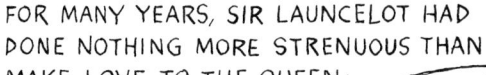

Sohrab and Rustum

HIS HEROIC STEED HAVING BEEN STOLEN, THE MIGHTY RUSTUM PURSUED THE THIEVES ON FOOT EVEN UNTO WHAT IS NOW THE U.S.S.R., TO BE WELCOMED BY THE KING OF GEORGIA.

Grrr...

Nice to see thee, Rust! How are things in Iran? Do not look so angry— stay and eat sheep's eyes with us.

AFTER MUCH FEASTING, RUSTUM WAS PERSUADED TO SLUMBER IN THE GUEST ROOM, WHEREIN BEFORE DAWN THERE CAME A VISIT FROM THE KING'S DAUGHTER.

What seekest thou from me, O bare one?

Three guesses, O hero! Peradventure Heaven will grant unto me a son like unto thee in valour, etc.

As an added inducement, I have found thy horse and it is moored without.

WHEN THE PRINCESS HAD BEEN OBLIGED, RUSTUM SADDLED HIS COURSER AND RODE BACK EVEN UNTO IRAN.

... for, as it is written, a woman hath but two legs.

NINE MOONS THEREAFTER

Such ferocity! Such hostility! The very double of his furious dad!

AT TEN YEARS OF AGE, THE LAD WAS SKILLED IN ALL THE ARTS OF WAR.

Mother, teach unto me my lineage; in other words, who is my old man? Describe him to me! If thou refuse, I will cleave thee in twain.

Ah, Sohrab, my son, what mother would not be proud at being thus threatened? His name is Rustum, and I know not whether he be bald, for he wore a hat.

So I am the son of Rustum? — a name known and feared throughout the uncivilised world!

I will lead an army of Turks against Iran, enthrone my father as the Shah— ...and then he will help me overthrow the Turks, and together we will slay everybody else! Farewell, mummy!

Go in peace, warlike boy!

BUT RUSTUM KNEW NOT OF SOHRAB'S EXISTENCE, LET ALONE OF HIS GRANDIOSE PLANS.

Rustum, an army of Turks approacheth, led by a tiny hero.

I will tiny hero him!

THEY BATTLED WITHOUT RESULT, NEITHER KNOWING THE OTHER.

Thou dost well, for a beardless tot! Let us rest, and resume hacking one another tomorrow.

I agree, O ancient flatulence, for I have beheld none like unto thee even at school.

THAT NIGHT

O Heathen Deity, grant me sufficient strength tomorrow to overcome this monstrous midget...

THE PRAYER OF RUSTUM WAS ANSWERED.

I am slain! I, Sohrab, the son of (gasp) Rustum...

The son of — ? Oh, damn.

MORAL: Carry identification, lest thou fall into the generation gap.

"The Luck-Child"

A POOR WOMAN GAVE BIRTH TO A BABY WITH THE MOST FORTUNATE PLANETARY CONFIGURATION EVER SEEN.

He has Mars in Scorpio?

And Venus in Aquarius! He can't miss!

ALL THE NEIGHBOURS THEREFORE CALLED HIM "THE LUCK-CHILD".

ONE DAY THE KING CAME RIDING THROUGH THE VILLAGE, IN DISGUISE.

What's all the excitement?

It's this baby! He has Mercury in Pisces!

With a start like that, he will undoubtedly grow up to marry the King's daughter.

The King's daughter, eh? Isn't that nice!

Give me the little chap. I will see that he gets a good education.

Oh, thank you, rich sir.

I **hate** babies with ideas above their station.

FRAGILE THIS WAY UP

MANY YEARS LATER, THE KING, NO LONGER IN DISGUISE, STOPPED AT A MILL.

And this is your son?

No, sir! We found him floating downstream, dried him off and brung him up.

I'm so lucky, it's silly.

Comb your hair, pet. The King wants you to deliver a letter to the Queen.

Dear Elsie, Have the bearer of this letter chopped up really small. Love, Jim

To the Queen

ON THE WAY TO THE PALACE, "THE LUCK-CHILD" SLEPT IN THE WOODS, WHERE HE WAS FOUND BY A BAND OF ROBBERS.

Chopped up small! I thought **we** were bloodthirsty.

Let's just re-write that.

Dear Elsie, Have the bearer of this letter ~~chopped up really small~~ MARRIED TO OUR DAUGHTER IMMEDIATELY. Love, Jim

To the Queen

My husband has gone off his rocker! Have you any money?

No, ma'am! But I have a moon in Taurus.

Your father apparently wants you to wed this pauper, dear. You must do as he commands.

What is your poverty-stricken name?

"The Luck-Child". I have Leo rising.

Cheeky!

Do you, Princess, take this penniless person?

Oh, yes! I would take two of him if possible.

Obviously a Gemini.

THE KING FINALLY RETURNED FROM HIS TRAVELS.

What! Married? Look here! First you have to slay a dragon and then you have to—

Bit late to make conditions, Dad.

Would you like "The Luck-Child" to do **your** chart?

MORAL: Good day for business transactions. Evening brings romance. Avoid elderly relatives.

St. George and Others

EGYPT WAS TERRORISED BY A DRAGON WHICH COULD BE APPEASED ONLY BY BEING GIVEN EACH DAY A BEAUTIFUL MAIDEN TO DEVOUR.

You must be joking! Take it away and bring me one with a cute little turned-up nose.

Hey, this is the Middle East! You'll be asking for blondes next.

LEARNING THAT THE KING'S DAUGHTER WAS ON THE LIST OF INTENDED VICTIMS, SAINT GEORGE SET SAIL FOR EGYPT, ARRIVING IN THE NICK OF TIME.

Bit small, aren't you? Nothing but a jumped-up lizard, really.

Just kill me, OK? Spare me the insults.

I don't know how to thank you enough! I suppose saints are forbidden carnal pleasures?

No — **priests** are forbidden those. Saints can do anything they like.

BUT THE KING OF MOROCCO DESIRED THE EGYPTIAN PRINCESS FOR HIMSELF.

She intends to turn Christian and marry the George person! Are you going to permit that, king of Egypt?

Is this true, daughter?

Yes. It's a fair Copt.

George, you haven't done anything for me since this morning. Run over to Persia and deliver this letter to the Sultan.

Glad to save you the postage.

"The bearer of this letter is a traitor to Islam." What the hell is Islam?

It is a religion so new that it does not yet exist, O Most High When Standing on a Table.

GEORGE WAS SENTENCED TO BE EATEN BY LIONS, BUT FOILED THEM WITH A MANOEUVRE HE HAD LEARNED AT THE HAGIOCRATIC INSTITUTE.

Plunge arms into tracheae and perform bronchoscopy.

HE THEN LANGUISHED IN PRISON FOR SEVEN YEARS, UNTIL A MEANS OF LIBERATION OCCURRED TO HIM.

Guard, St. George has escaped, disguised as me!

By Allah, you **do** look like him! I had better release you, that you may pursue him.

Arab horses are very good, I have to admit.

Now to go to Morocco and kill the King, who forcibly married my beloved while I was on the wild goose chase to Persia.

AN EMOTIONALLY FRAUGHT REUNION

Forget about slaying my husband! He isn't worth it!

I could have sworn he was.

YEARS LATER, IN OXSHOTT

I'll never get used to this climate! Why did we flee **here**, of all places?

I've **explained** it to you! I have to be the damned patron saint.

MORAL: Kiss the girls (making them cry is optional).

DADDYKINS

THERE ONCE LIVED A QUEEN WHO WAS THE MOST BEAUTIFUL WOMAN IN THE WORLD; BUT SHE WAS MORTALLY ILL WITH AN INCURABLE ELECTRA COMPLEX.

Medical science is baffled, dear lady.

We have tried everything: leeches, free association...

Fools! My father was worth ten of you!

You see? No hope.

I am going to die soon, husband. Promise that you will not remarry a woman less gorgeous than myself.

Why?

Daddykins would have wanted it that way.

TEN YEARS WENT BY AFTER THE QUEEN'S DEATH. (OF COURSE, THEY WOULD HAVE GONE BY ANYWAY.)

Ah, daughter, you have grown into a fascinating woman. You remind me of your mother.

Thank you, daddykins.

Good God! Why not?

With respect, Majesty, marrying one's own daughter is forbidden.

What about Lot?

Lot was drunk.

I'll get drunk.

Damn it all, chaps, I made a promise to my wife!

But, daddykins—

I do not care that for recessive genes! Name your wedding present.

SNAP

A dress made from the pelts of every terrified little furry species.

THE PRINCESS MADE THIS REQUEST IN ORDER TO BUY TIME, BUT THE KING COMMANDED HIS HUNTSMEN TO TRAP AND SKIN AS THEY HAD NEVER TRAPPED AND SKINNED BEFORE.

Why are you running? Nobody wears amphibian garments.

They put frogs on pyjamas, don't they?

A perfect fit! We will be wed tomorrow. At my age there is no time to lose, although, so far, knock wood ···

BONK

...And that is why I have run away to hide in the woods, dear little field mouse.

You have the gall to come here wearing my father, to complain about your father?

THE ANIMALS, IN REVENGE, LED THE PRINCESS TO A TRAP.

Look at that, Arthur — a skunkmole.

Or is it a beavervole?

Do not skin me! I am a person!

Heavens, a talking weaselshrew — I thought they were extinct.

Ah, there you are. For a moment I feared you had run away. It seems (I have just read your late mother's diary) that I am not your father after all.

You are, in fact, the daughter of your grandfather.

Dearly beloved and others···

Which makes me — let me see — your half-me see — your half-stepbrother-in-law, perhaps?

Perhaps, half-stepkins.

MORAL: The child is father to the man, but beyond that it is very difficult to trace one's ancestry.

Adventures of Samson

SAMSON'S WEAKNESS: PHILISTINE WOMEN.

I now pronounce you hulking idiot and wife.

See me later, Best Man.

She's with your **friend**, Samson! Better a friend than a total stranger, no?

Moan Moan

Have you met my younger daughter?

REVENGE: BURNING THE PHILISTINES' FIELDS.

There! **Now** she'll be sorry.

This may well mark the end of my first marriage.

RESISTING ARREST.

THE JAWBONE OF AN ASS

CLUNK

THUMP

997 — you shouldn't — 998 — make me — 999 — lose my temper — 1000. And that's all for today.

LOCKED IN THE CITY WHILE PATRONISING A HARLOT.

Leaving so soon? I'm only vaguely bruised.

Nice gates. I'll take them home.

MARRIAGE WITH DELILAH.

You again? Some people never learn.

Don't forget: hard cash for hard facts.

Do, you, Musclehead, take this spy···

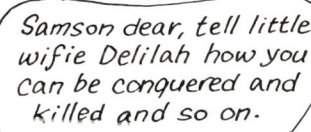

Samson dear, tell little wifie Delilah how you can be conquered and killed and so on.

I have to be tied up with sort of special ropes.

You lied! Shame on you!

SNAP   Hee hee!   SNAP

SNAP

SNAP

SNAP

If you really **loved** me, you would tell me how to kill you and so on.

Oh, all **right**! Just stop **nagging**! It's my hair.

TONSORIAL TREACHERY.

Back and sides go bare, go bare···

snore

SNIP SNIP SNIP

CAPTURE.

You guarantee that this bald person is Samson?

You won't hurt him, will you? I kind of liked the big lug.

We'll just put out his eyes and then play it by ear.

NEW HAIR AND FINAL VENGEANCE.

Now to pull down their temple — come to my aid, O stubble!

If I kill 3000, that beats my previous record.

MORAL: Keep your hair on.

61

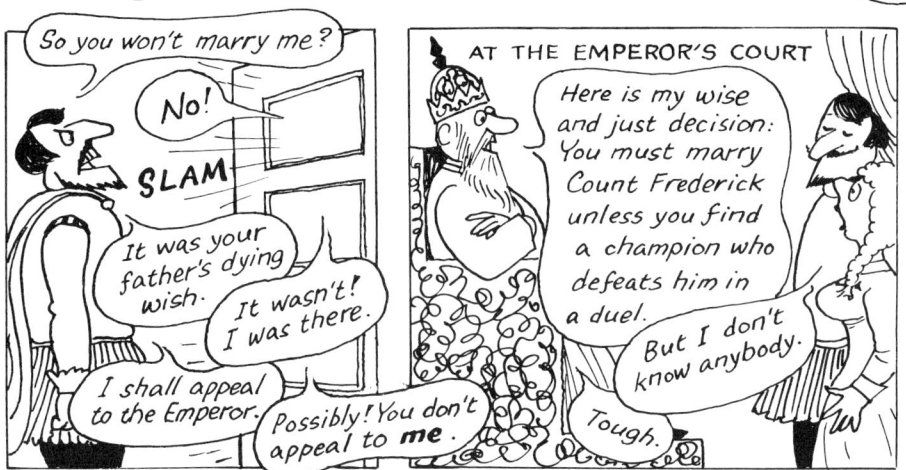

MORAL: Never mind what the neighbours think.

The Lady Ragnell

KING ARTHUR WAS TRICKED INTO CHALLENGING THE ENCHANTED SIR GROMER SOMER.

I suddenly feel so cowardly! That isn't like me at all.

It is the evil magic of your evil sister, the evil Queen Morgana le Fay! But I will spare your life if —

— you return in a twelvemonth and tell me what it is that women most desire! Should you give the wrong answer, you will suffer disgrace! and death! — followed by indescribable torture.

ARTHUR RETURNED A YEAR LATER, ACCOMPANIED BY SIR GAWAIN.

Look, uncle, a hideous lady.

Stay!

By my troth, nephew, she might sour a whole quart of cream.

I, the Lady Ragnell, know the answer to the riddle — but one of you must become my husband.

Well, of course, I am already married.

Goodbye, world.

Agreed? Very well, the answer is (whisper whisper)

No! Really?

Well? What do women most desire?

Love? Money? Power? Ginger ale?

No! No! No! Prepare to die.

All right then, it's (whisper whisper)

What? That is the right answer! I am undone!

THE WEDDING WAS A JOYLESS AFFAIR.

Do you, Gawain, take this loathsome creature···

I — ugh — do.

Time for bed, dearie! Are you not going to kiss your lovely bride?

Of course.

Stomach, try to think about something else.

Well done, brave lord! You have released me from my enchantment!

Whoopee! Something actually went right!

But tell me: what do women most desire?

Having our backs scratched. Ah····

Obvious, when you think about it.

SCRATCH SCRATCH

MORAL: Marry a witch. She may change into a beautiful lady. (Too many of you have been doing it the wrong way round.)

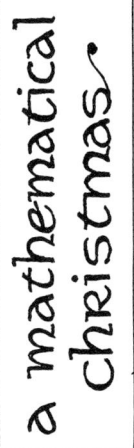